MR. PEPINO'S CABBAGE

Diane Wilmer and Anna Currey

Illustrated by Anna Currey

GALLERY BOOKS
An Imprint of W. H. Smith Publishers Inc.
112 Madison Avenue
New York City 10016

High on the mountainside, overlooking the valley, is Santa Maria, the prettiest town in the world. Mr. Pepino lives here, with his wife and their little daughter, Matilda.

Down in the valley the townspeople have their
gardens.
This is where they grow their vegetables:
big cabbages, fat tomatoes,
green beans, and sweet peas.

In a field behind the gardens lives a family of rabbits. Lots and lots of them. Matilda loves the rabbits very much.

One day she sneaked up to the rabbits' field and fed them the best vegetables she could find. "This is a secret," she whispered. "You mustn't tell anybody about it or I'll get into trouble with my papa."

But once the rabbits had tasted the delicious
vegetables they were hungry for more.
"Come on," said Lupino, the greediest rabbit of
them all. "Let's help ourselves."
And they all wriggled through the fence and
nibbled and gnawed at everything in sight.

Lupino spotted a big, fat cabbage.
"Oh my!" he sighed. "That's the biggest cabbage
I've *ever* seen."

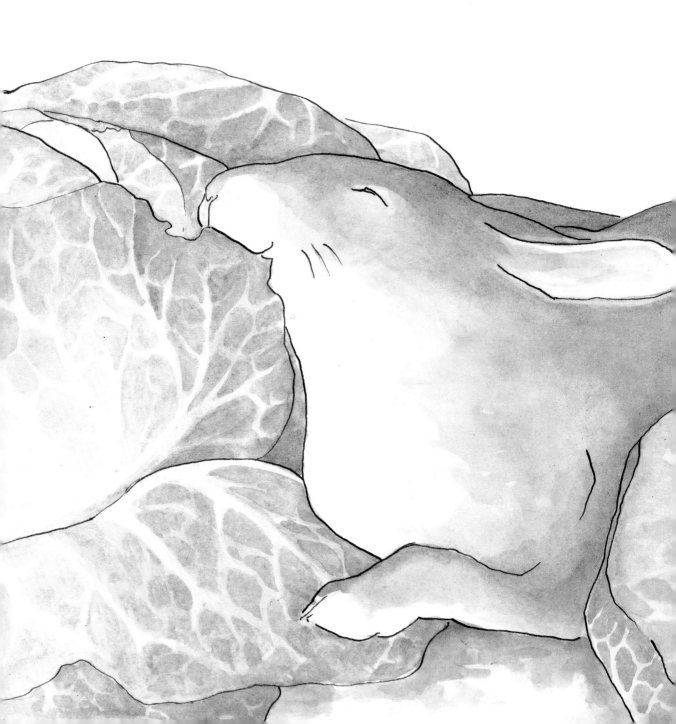

He munched and crunched until there was hardly any cabbage left at all.
He didn't know it was Mr. Pepino's cabbage.
The one he'd grown from a seed.
He didn't know it was the one Mr. Pepino had been keeping for the town show!

The next day Mr. Pepino went down to his garden and all that was left of his beautiful cabbage was one leaf.

"Mama Mia!" he roared. "Who has done this terrible thing?"

The rabbits peeped out at Mr. Pepino.

"You!" he shouted.

"It was you! Well, you'll have to go!"

Mr. Pepino told his wife what had happened. Then
he shouted at Matilda.
"We'll have to get rid of those rabbits!"
he bellowed.
Matilda cried. Her mother cried.

And so did Mr. Pepino. "Boo-hoo!" he sobbed.
"Now I'll never win a prize at the town show."

Matilda felt terrible.
"Come on," said her mother. "Let's go down to the market."
But everybody in town was laughing and chattering about the show.

"Have you seen Mr. Pepino's cabbage!" they
said. "It's so big and beautiful. It must win a prize
in the show tomorrow."
Matilda started to cry all over again. "Oh dear,"
she sobbed. "It's all my fault. What can I do?"

Mrs. Pepino took Matilda down to the garden to pick some beans for dinner, but there they found the rabbits eating Uncle Costello's best peas.
"Oh! You bad rabbits!" shouted Matilda.
All the rabbits stopped eating and stared at her.
"First you eat my father's best cabbage and now you're eating my uncle's prize peas!

There'll be nothing left for the show. My papa will be very angry and you will have to leave Santa Maria."

The rabbits did not want to leave the valley.
"Now, which of you ate my father's big
cabbage?" said Matilda.
All the rabbits pointed at Lupino.
"Greedy boy!" scolded Matilda. "No wonder
you're so fat."

Matilda stared at Lupino…then she had a
brilliant idea.
"Do you know, you're so fat you're big enough to
win a prize at the town show," she said.

"But Lupino isn't a cabbage," said Mrs. Pepino.
"He's a rabbit."
"I know," said Matilda, "but he's twice as big
as a cabbage and much more beautiful too. I'll put
him in the Pet Show."

The next day the bells rang out across the hillside
and all the people came running to the town show.
They brought bread and cakes.
Eggs and ham.
Goats and sheep.
Cheese and cream.
Cats and dogs.
And the best fruits and vegetables you have
ever seen.

Everybody wanted to win a prize, but only the best could win. Only the very, very best.
Uncle Costello won a prize for his peas.
Mrs. Pompinelli got one for her beautiful cake.

And Matilda won a big box of chocolates for her
pretty painting.
Everybody was happy.
Everybody but Mr. Pepino.

"Now for the Pet Show!" called the judge.
Matilda lifted Lupino out of his box and gave him
to her father.
"Here, take him," she whispered.
"No, no, no!" cried her father. "He doesn't belong to me."
"But he ate your best cabbage and he's really very
sorry," said Matilda.

Mr. Pepino looked at Lupino.
The naughty rabbit wriggled his ears and twitched
his nose.
"Oh, please Papa, put him in the Pet Show,"
begged Matilda.

So that's what Mr. Pepino did.
There were cats, dogs, a turkey, some ducks,
a rooster, two goats and lots of rabbits.
The turkey came in third and a duck came in second.
But the first prize went to the biggest and most
beautiful rabbit at the show.

It was LUPINO!
"Three cheers for Mr. Pepino," cried the judge.
"Hurray! Hurray! Hurray!" yelled the crowd.
"Mama Mia," said Mr. Pepino. "At last I've won a prize!"

Mr. Pepino was *so* happy. He polished his cup until it gleamed.

"Please can the rabbits stay, Papa?" asked Matilda.

Mr. Pepino thought about it for a long time. Then he smiled.

"They can stay if they stop *stealing* our vegetables," he said. "You can give them a few each day. But tell them to stay out of the garden."

"I will, Papa," said Matilda. "I promise I will."

So, every day Matilda feeds the rabbits and they do as they are told. She brings them green beans, sweet peas and fat tomatoes.

"Only the best," says Matilda.

And the rabbits nod back at her. They know they always get the very best in town.

This edition first published in the United States in 1989 by Gallery Books, an imprint of W.H. Smith Publishers, Inc., 112 Madison Avenue, New York, New York 10016. Produced for Gallery Books by Joshua Morris Publishing, Inc. in association with William Collins Sons & Co. Ltd. Text copyright © 1989 by William Collins Sons & Co. Ltd. Illustrations copyright © 1989 by Anna Currey. All rights reserved. ISBN 0-8317-4424-3 Printed in Hong Kong.